WHAT IT TAKES
TO FIND YOUR
True Love

WHAT IT TAKES TO FIND YOUR
True Love

BONNIE

To order additional copies of this book, contact:
Xlibris
1-888-795-4274
www.Xlibris.com
Orders@Xlibris.com
708921

CONTENTS

Dedication

I want to dedicate this book to my dear husband. He was the driving encouragement in getting this book written. He is the love of my life and with him we found true love! We got married in 2014. Together we have learned to put away the past and to move on to the future!

Chapter One

Introduction

The main objective in writing this book is to hopefully help others avoid making the mistakes I've made in finding a true love. This is a process that takes a lot of soul searching and honest self-appraisal as to what you want from others and of what others can expect from you. You have to delve deep into your psyche and face your weaknesses. I hope you will be willing to do these things so that you can avoid the years of mistakes that I made because I didn't take the time to do this until my back was against the wall!

I'm going to go throughout my entire life, describing the types of relationships I had with various people, and how these relationships shaped my personality and character, and eventually affected the relationships I ended up in because of it. I hope that you can appreciate the myriad experiences I endured and/or enjoyed.

Chapter Two

Where It All Began

Have you ever found yourself in a relationship and asked yourself, "What am I doing here?" Well, a lot of us have done that, and like some of us, we've found ourselves there a number of times.

My previous relationship was not going well; I was feeling stuck, and not knowing how to get out of it, my partner died suddenly with no warning.

So that's how I found myself on a journey to find myself. I was 52 years old and I had spent my life always thinking of other people and living according to their needs and wants. I had never thought about what I would like out of life, or what I wanted for myself. I had no clue as to where I should start!

So with the help of my social worker, from whom I needed support and guidance, I started on an exciting journey.

At this point, I had no interest in getting into any relationship. I needed to find myself for the first time in my life! I had to ask myself a lot of questions, like "what did I like; what did I dislike? What did I want out of life? What made me happy, sad? What made me laugh, cry, angry? What did I enjoy doing? What kind of friends did I want to have? What kind of friend did I want to be? Who am I? Who do I want to be?" Just start finding out what makes me me!

So, you ask, how did I come up with all these ideas? Because of all my past relationships that made up my life-parents, brothers, and sisters, friends and boyfriends.

When my boyfriend died I was at the lowest point in my life and I had had some really low times before.

2. Tim 4:16 "No one came to my support, but everyone deserted me. May it not be held against them. But the lord stood at my side and gave me strength."

Everybody just left me. One day I said to God, "All I have is you" and it opened my eyes to the fact that all I ever needed was Jesus the Lord! He was everything and the only one I needed. I went back to my roots from the early '90's, when I became born again. Nobody could give me what the Lord could. The creator of the universe and of all life was my friend and lover. And from that day on things started getting lighter and I felt more peaceful.

Chapter Three

Infancy to First Grade

Before my birth, my mother had had a previous miscarriage, and when she was pregnant with me, in order to not lose me also, her doctor recommended she stay in bed, which she did for a few months. Two months before I was born my dad lost his job.

Then I was born about 6 weeks premature. I had to stay in the hospital in an incubator until I was strong enough to go home. For two weeks I stayed there, no mom or dad to come and see me- the nurses would call them every day to let them know how I was doing.

I was born the third child, having a ten year old brother and a five year old sister. I was the baby of the family my first five years.

Our family was Catholic, so we went to church every Sunday and every holy day. My older brother and sister were close, so they did their own things together.

My brother babysat me usually on Sunday mornings while the rest of the family went to church. I was too small to go. I remember some Sundays I would wake up while the family was in church, and I would be calling for my mother, being scared and alone. I also didn't attend kindergarten because I was so small and shy.

My older sister and I got really close and spent a lot of time together. Then when I was five, my mom had my baby brother. I was jealous of him from day one, but I also became protective of him because he seemed vulnerable. Even though mom favored him, she and dad were too strict with him (I thought). He was so shy and so sweet, but he also had learned very young how to irk me and have mom on his side. It was a complex and confusing relationship. I guess it became a way for me to live-protecting my tormentors. Try to figure that out!

All the years I was growing up, my mother repeatedly told me that I was very expensive when I was born! Two weeks in the hospital was expensive, especially since my dad was unemployed, and there were five of us to take care of. Four hundred dollars was a lot of money in 1955.

My dad played the accordion, and there was a song he played, when I was three or four years old, that would always make me cry. There was something about that song that made me feel sad, but he would keep playing it anyway.

Since my mother wasn't with me the first two weeks of my life, I've never had that bonding that mothers and babies have right at the start. I think this definitely affected my entire life. All my life I've had a hard time really getting close to people-that's why I've always preferred to be alone and entertain myself. I only like one on one relationships. If I'm in a group of more people I feel alienated-it's just a fact of my life.

Chapter Four

Indoctrination

My siblings and I were then sent to private school, and teachers were abusive both physically and emotionally. I was always being punished for other classmate's disruptive behavior. This caused resentment in me. I didn't know how to speak up for myself, and my teachers wouldn't even let me tell them what really happened.

Having to be six or older for first grade, I started school in September of my sixth year. My seventh birthday was in January. My being older than most of my classmates kind of set me apart from them. I always felt more mature than them.

I was very shy and the teachers scared me. I thought they were mean. And we had to attend church every day of the week before school started. The teachers were very strict and they demanded to be shown respect by all of us. We had to stand in line by our height so I was always first in line-talk about stress!

Since I didn't feel like I fit in with my classmates, I found other interests. One day instead of going out to recess, I stayed in and played "teacher." The teacher caught me going from desk to desk, handing out sheets of paper. Another time the teacher found me cleaning out students desks, and she told me both times that I have to go outside and play with the other children. So it went.

In second grade I had an old crabby teacher. She used to tell us stories about how the Nazi's tortured people over in Germany. She was physically abusive to me. She did things like spank me in front of the class because I didn't answer loud enough. I was terrified of her!

Then she would let students wear Chinese hats if they only got two wrong on the math test, except when it happened to me, then only students getting one wrong got to wear the hat! I could never do anything right for her. Talk about giving a kid a complex!

Another thing I need to mention is that I had to walk over a mile to school and back again each day. Rain or shine, hot or cold, I had to walk to school. Sometimes there were bullies threatening us.

When I was eight, my baby sister was born. Since I was so much older than her, I didn't really feel affected. Mom asked me to announce her birth to the school principle. I kind of resented having to do it because I was so shy, but I did it, but it seemed to me that the principle really couldn't have cared less! I still don't understand why my older sister hadn't been asked to do it.

Third grade was even worse than second grade. We had a lay teacher and she favored certain kids in school. One girl kept talking to another, and she was never punished. But when I turned around because this girl was bothering me the teacher gave her permission to hit me on the head with a ruler.

So this went on for a long time. I started getting dizzy spells because of this abuse and started going home sick. I finally told my mother about this and she had a talk with the teacher, but the damage had been done by then.

Then thank God in fourth grade, I got a teacher that helped me get through difficulties. Finally someone cared! This teacher read us a story in a novel about wildlife and nature, and I found this very soothing.

Also, my big sister and I spent a lot of time singing songs with the transistor radio: here's a story about some of them:

"Singing Memories"

My big sister and a friend and I are sitting on the lawn in front of our childhood home. We are singing a little ditty, "on the good ship lollipop" and I forgot a lot of the words, but we are just full of joy singing this song.

Other songs we sang are hidden deep within my memory, but I know that if I focus on this experience, the memories could surface. Right now picturing this, my emotions are here, right under the surface. Also our school's song for sports went "Thunder, thunder, thunderation," it's been so long since I thought of this.

My sister moved two hundred miles away to be close to her son. But since she's been gone, I feel like I lost a part of myself. All of our lives we were so close. She was my big sister, but we were also best friends. I feel kind of lost without her near. I've been trying to find a new friend, but my efforts have not been fruitful. How can you find someone like that after being "a part of her for 56 years?"

I just feel lonely and kind of lost, really. I'm not sure of where I can go from here. At this age it is much more difficult to find a bond with someone new. Maybe I'm too old for this "losing" two people that I loved dearly in the past five years. I guess I'm kind of a slow learner when it comes to separating from people I've known, and loved, and lived with, and enjoyed activities with.

I need to "grow new arms", but it's hard; it's difficult, but maybe I need to relax and just open my heart to myself and let go of expectations of others. I need to learn to live and leave the worries to God. He will lead me to where he wants me to be. "But", how do you learn to do this after you've lived almost six decades, over half a century? Lord give me new wings so that I can soar and reach new destinations, and to find those parts of myself I have never known!

As a child I loved reading books, and that's how I spent most of my free time, all year long. Summer vacations were spent checking books out of the library, and reading them in the shade in the yard. I loved books, and it was my great escape from life's stress!

At home I was responsible for my younger brother and sister. When I got home from school, I was expected to pick up after them, and to do some housekeeping. If my siblings did something wrong, I was responsible. I had a lot of responsibility for my young age.

Our family spent a lot of nights watching TV; I Love Lucy, wrestling, Lawrence Welk and such. Weekends my mom and dad went out dancing and drinking. We never knew what mood they'd be in when they came home. Life at home was even more chaotic than school and the nuns. There was nothing stable in our lives.

Fifth and sixth grade are kind of a blur to me. My older brother had come back from the army, and he had gotten married. So there was a baby on the way, and he and his wife had moved to another state to be close to her parents. So I wrote letters to them regularly-I missed him. He was a very interesting guy who loved music, and he was always involved in fun activities.

Every summer vacation from school was a lot of fun running barefoot in the neighborhood. I grew up across the street from a Fairground, so there was baseball, and hopscotch, and running hurdles through the sheep and pig pens.

There was no end of fun things to do; playing hide and seek among the sumac hedges; climbing trees; riding bike everywhere. We'd swing on the swings there, and we would compete as to who could swing the highest without flipping over the top bar. I loved spinning on the small merry-go-round. I'd go so fast I would get high and stagger off.

As it got closer to going back to school, I started getting excited about starting a new grade. I looked forward to getting my books and my new school supplies! Fall was my favorite time of the year. It was the start of new beginnings, time for learning and expanding.

The end of the summer was kicked off by the fair. I spent so much time at the fair that workers, thinking I was an orphan, gave me free rides. Free rides and specials until one day my sister came to get me for supper and one of the men heard her tell me to come home. That was the end of free rides!

Another thing I loved on summer days was lying on the grass and finding shapes in the clouds. And it was fun watching the shade roll across the ground-watching the shade roll down the block slowly and pass over me.

I loved going to my grandma's farm and taking walks through the woods with my dad. He'd point out trees, and plants, and birds, and animals. That was our special time together. My relationship with my dad was the only stable one I had with a man until I met my husband. Dad could be depended on, and he didn't change like other people. He never surprised me with an unexpected reaction, which I needed badly in my life.

My relationship with my mom was mostly one of learning to do housework and cook and sew. She taught me a lot. But our relationship was always kind of rocky, because I didn't cow-tow to her domineering ways and I had a mind of my own, which she resented. I got pushed around enough at school, so I learned to stand my ground at home.

On summer vacation my older sister and I liked to pretend we were famous singers and sing with the radio. And we loved to play school and put on plays of our own. We had many ways of entertaining ourselves to stay out of mom's way.

Also since each of us were five years apart, that made a lot of differences in our lives. Like school, friends, and interests.

When I was ten, I started working babysitting for neighbors or doing housework. I gave all the money to mom and dad to help them.

Chapter Five

Rebellion

Near the end of sixth grade, my parents bought a brand new house, and we moved to a neighboring town. The neighborhood was a lot nicer and well-groomed. My older sister and I shared a bedroom. We loved our new house!

Brand new! Our old house had been rebuilt by my dad and uncle, and the upstairs we slept in was never finished. No finished ceiling or walls and no insulation. We had frozen every winter! What a change!

My first boyfriend

I was thirteen, and he was seventeen. My sisters' friend's brother. He gave me his ring to wear on a chain. He was very shy. I remember the first time we touched-in a movie theatre-and the electricity I felt as our fingers touched. He never even kissed me. We just did activities with our sisters at our house. He was a momma's boy and he broke up with me over the phone. I was so broken hearted! I cried for year's afterword. I started hating men because they hurt.

When I was a teenager, I loved the Righteous Brothers because of the love I had experienced at thirteen. I knew the pain of love lost. I had learned a hard lesson by thirteen. It's here today and gone tomorrow. I don't think anyone knew how much I was suffering. He was my first love, and it hurt me deeply when he said he didn't love me anymore, influenced by his mother.

He had let me down, and I didn't want to hurt like that again! So I just planned my own life. I did a lot of reading to ease my pain, and listened to the radio, and wrote stories. I did a lot of artistic work and drawings. I started spending more time alone. I had nothing in common with my peers-they seemed so childish compared to me. I had loved and lost at a young age. I wasn't a kid anymore!

Also with a new house came new friends in the neighborhood. A bunch of us played softball in the empty lot in the neighborhood. I became a good pitcher. There was also a park three blocks away where we played baseball.

This was also a stressful time for me, being the new kid in the neighborhood, and in school. I started spending more time by myself, reading novels, putting jigsaw puzzles together, journaling, sketching, painting and listening to the radio. When I was alone I felt relaxed and no one had expectations of me.

When I started ninth grade I attended junior high school- the first public school I ever attended. I made friends with a girl whose name was the same as mine, and she had a friend. The three of us started hanging around together.

I had evolved from a shy and obedient child to a rebellious teenager, and I had become more outspoken after all the tension I had lived under. So my mother didn't know what to do with me when I got angry, so she let me do whatever I wanted. If I stayed out roaming around with my girlfriends, she didn't say much. Sometimes I would come home around 2:30 or 3:30 in the morning. Back then we didn't even have to lock our doors at night. Life was pretty safe.

At fifteen, my doctor gave me tranquilizers to help me deal with stress. So I got into that habit for quite a few years. Plus I had gotten into heavy drinking with the family often. Every occasion and holiday the booze was flowing with all of us. It was a mess.

Then when I started high school, I spent more time with my girlfriends playing hooky, roaming the halls at school etc. Since I had little motivation from my parents to go to school, I dropped out officially right after my sixteenth birthday. I was depressed, nobody really cared what I did, and I started spending more time with my older sister, who had gotten married when I was thirteen.

My sister and I had always been close, and I had always hung out with her and her friends. I liked older people. I always thought my classmates were immature-flirting with boys and going to beer parties was childish. It just wasn't my thing-I liked older kids and adults. I felt I had more in common with them than with kids my age.

I had been reading the newspaper and paying attention to the news since I was eleven or twelve. Current events were important to me, and there was a lot going on in the world and in America back then. Boy does that bring back memories!

When I was seventeen I had my first sexual experience. My girlfriend and I took the Greyhound bus to a big city, and we got a hotel room at a hotel downtown. We ran into a black guy by the bus depot, and he took us out for a ride. He went to his friend's house and picked him up. Then we went to the other guy's house, and I ended up having sex with him. It was my first time and I was high on tranquilizers. Later they dropped us off at the hotel, and he called me the next morning to see how I was. Four months later he called me again to see how I was. He was still calling me when I was twenty two and living with another boyfriend.

Later that year I met another guy through my girlfriend, and we got pretty serious. We had fun together, and in October he invited me to come and live with him up north, where he had gotten a job. So with my mother's permission, I went there with all my belongings. We were staying in a trailer on a horse ranch. The next afternoon, five cop cars drove up to the house. This was like déjà vu to me. I had a dream of this happening. The cops asked me if I had known that he was an escaped convict. Then they took me to the bus depot downtown, and I had to wait until midnight to catch the bus home.

During the hours waiting in the depot guys were propositioning me. It was a horrible experience! I thought "This could only happen to me!" I was miserable, and I couldn't wait to get home again.

I really became a loner after that experience. I spent a lot of time journaling and writing and reading novels to heal my wounds. Once in a while my girlfriend would call me up and ask if I wanted to double date. I would go once in a while although I didn't care for the kind of guys she knew, but it was better than being alone. So life went on.

Chapter Six

Being Independent

My first job at eighteen was working on an assembly line in a factory, doing manual labor. I didn't know any better, my dad was a laborer. It was hard, physical, work, but we had fun.

In late November I decided to move to another state since my boyfriend was going to get out of prison. I had kept in touch with him. I got a job as a nanny and housekeeper, and I did quite well for a while. But being far from family was hard on me, so I moved back home, and lost touch with the boyfriend.

It wasn't long before I began asking myself "How could I have missed my family?" Living at home again was a pain. I got a job and started paying rent to my parents again (I never lived free with them). And then came the knocking on the bathroom door when I was taking a shower, and my mother stating that "You've been in there long enough". My rent was paying over half the house payment, but obviously it didn't pay for the water! So as soon as I could, I found a house to rent with my sister who was divorced now and had a two year old son. For most of our lives we were almost inseparable, so we thought it would work out. First problem was I had to lend her half of the deposit.

Next her boyfriend, moved in with us without discussing it with me. He didn't help pay one-third of the rent, just the phone bill and some food. What could I say? I had just left one bad situation for another!

So with all this crap in my life, and people taking advantage of me, I had a nervous breakdown, and ended up in the hospital for two weeks. Shortly after I moved back with mom and dad.

I went to group therapy for a few months, and got the support I needed. I also got a job at a hospital through a government program, and things started looking up. I dated now and then, and I also found a place of my own.

I was happy being on my own again, without people telling me what to do. I also had a steady boyfriend. But when he didn't want a commitment, I ended the relationship. It felt like I was doing all the giving, and he was doing all the taking. I felt empowered ending that relationship, and not just "putting up with" anymore. I needed to be in charge of my life, and I needed to call the shots. I had been short changing myself long enough!

I decided if they weren't serious about me, and they didn't have what it takes to be in a relationship, then I didn't have the time for them. I felt very freed and emboldened by this! I was in charge of my life, and it was about time.

I was still going to school to earn my high school diploma, and I started working at the laundry company with my sister. So we spent a lot of time together after work, going to the bar with our friend to have a few drinks before going home. I spent a lot of weekends and holidays with family, and I cooked a lot of meals for them, which I always loved doing.

Chapter Seven

Starting College

Shortly after I met someone, a neighbor. He had come to America one year earlier, and we liked each other's company. So we moved in together, to save on rent. He was working a labor job and so was I. Also, I was still working on my high school diploma, getting ready for college, which I had planned when I was in ninth grade. I was twenty one years old now.

He and I shared an apartment, but we kind of had separate lives. I cooked a lot of American food for us after work, and he cooked his food often, since he said that American food gave him a "heavy belly".

He and I spent the summer fishing after work. We caught a lot of fish, and he showed me how to cook fish his native way, which was delicious!

A lot of weekends I spent with my younger brother. We were like best friends. We'd go driving out in the country, drinking beer in the car, and playing loud rock-n-roll music. We had fun!

I finally got my GED, and started college. I was twenty three years old. At thirteen I had told a teacher that I wanted to study psychology, but my boyfriend said that if I was going to spend money going to school, I should take something that's going to get me a good paying job as fast as possible.

So I started Business College, studying accounting. I had to attend six classes a day, plus I had to work twenty hours a week to pay for rent and living expenses. Well, that didn't give me time to do all the homework that I had each day. I became severely depressed, and I had to quit school.

In the meantime my brother had gone into the army, and I missed him. For the next two years we wrote letters back and forth, telling each other how things were going.

Then I went to the university and signed up for what I truly wanted, psychology. I loved college-the classes, the environment, and I got a job in the library (I loved libraries!)

My boyfriend and I moved to separate living places. I lived in a beauty college dorm. I attended school, and worked in the library. Then in the fall, I got a work study job in the president's office. There I met, a born again Christian, a fellow student, and we rented an apartment with two other students.

She was good inspiration for me because I was searching for god at that time. Having three roommates was hard to deal with. One of them wanted everything her way.

Then in late May of 1980, through friends I had made in an on-campus AA group, I decided to go through treatment at the Hospital. During the thirty days of treatment, my counselors kept my boyfriend away from me. They said he was toxic to me because he was so demanding and physically abusive.

After treatment I went to a halfway house. It was a huge mansion on a lake with an indoor pool and a great room with floor to ceiling windows facing a lake. It was pretty fancy. I lived there with thirty other recovering women. We had group in the morning after breakfast, which we took turns putting on, both the group and the breakfast, and then a bus took us to downtown for work or to look for work. I spent the day applying for jobs, and then at 5 p.m. the bus took us back to the house.

When I went to the halfway house the people at the hospital didn't tell my boyfriend where I went. Living with thirty women could be trying at times, but overall I had good roommates. Eventually he found out where I was, and I started seeing him when I went to the city. Shortly after, I decided to go back to home with him. He had started school studying accounting. I got a job at the County Highway Department at the court house and I worked there for almost a year, and then I got laid off. I worked as a receptionist/bookkeeper.

I planned on going back to college to study psychology, but my boyfriend had graduated and was having a hard time getting an accounting job because computers were coming in and he needed to know how to use them.

Being so far from my family, he became more abusive towards me. I loved college, I loved my classes, and I became an A student. I got a job working in periodicals in the library again!

I was doing very well in school, but he was having difficulty with the computer classes. So he encouraged me to study computer science with him, and because I was an A student, we thought I would be good at computer science and I was!

I started taking computer courses and business management courses, and I did very well. But I ended up writing essays and other papers for his classes, since he wasn't very good at it. I resented doing it, but he always said, "It's for us and our future," so I continued this for four years besides all my own school work.

When the tension and abuse got to be too much, I would leave him and go back to my family. He would come and follow me, begging me to come back. Since I didn't get any support from my family-they didn't want any trouble for them, I went back each time. It was a no win situation, so I would go back and continue school.

When I got a job at the college, I made some new friends. They would help me out when I was having difficulties with my boyfriend, and I did some fun things with them outside of school.

His and my relationship had been rocky from the start. We were more like brother and sister. We also had a symbiotic relationship where when one of us was weak, the other would hold him/her up. Not so good. There was a lot of tension and expectations on both sides. And when those expectations weren't filled, there were angry outbursts and physical abuse on both our sides. When the tension became unbearable I would run away to my family. I loved him deeply-I just couldn't live without him and vice-versa.

Chapter Eight

Being on Top of the World

Finally after four years of hard work I was ready to graduate. My family had been causing me some trouble, so I just cut off totally from them shortly before graduating.

I got an internship at a large insurance company, and I was on my way with computer programming. Getting used to living in the big city was a breeze for me. I was on top of the world!

But my boyfriend, still in college, and looking for a job, would have me stay up late typing cover letters for his job searching. It was always about him! He didn't care if I wasn't getting enough sleep!

He finally got hired by a company in another town, so he moved there. That gave me more freedom to enjoy my job, and my personal life. My half hour commute each way to and from work became too much, and the cost of parking each day downtown was very expensive. So when the subsidiary company hired me for January, 1986, I moved. Then I took the city bus to and from work each day to save time and money.

So I attended a lot of entertainment venues with new friends and I was really enjoying life.

On weekends my boyfriend and I would take turns visiting each other. We did a lot of dining out, but he still would get angry and abusive with me. It was crazy. After three more years of this going on, I couldn't take it anymore! I finally told him that if he couldn't love me just the way I am, then he needs to look for someone else! This was after twelve years together. It was time for me to move on with my life. So the next morning we said goodbye, and he left. The relationship had died.

Right along this time came another boyfriend. I thought, "Great, I'll have a white American boyfriend, and we will have a lot in common". It never happened! He was the perfect man, right? Wrong! He proposed to me on his knee in front of my family. It was all an act! He never even bought the ring, I did.

He was verbally abusive to me. We only stayed together about ten months and he was even crazier than my previous boyfriend. Also he stole thousands of dollars from me. I found out much later. Thank God he walked out the door one night, and I said, "Good riddance!"

My ex-boyfriend came and lent me $250 to go back to be with my family, and to find a place to live. So I went home and found a family friend. There was a room for rent in the house she was living. So I made arrangements to move there.

My dad, my brother, and my brother-in-law came and moved all my stuff out of my apartment, and helped me move back home. This was October of 1989.

Chapter Nine

Coming Home and Falling in the Rabbit Hole

Here I was, back home after ten years. It was both a good thing and a bad thing. All my dreams had fallen apart. I went from being on top of the world to being in hell. I was sort of happy to be back at home with the family. I had been gone for ten years, with college and working in the cities. It was pretty depressing due to the circumstances, but I adjusted like always.

I had to put up with roommates again. Four of them in the house, but I had the basement with my own kitchen, so that helped. Later my older sister shared the basement with me. We would have arguments now and then. I needed time to myself and had a "do not disturb" sign on my door and she took it personally. It had nothing to do with her; it was just a phase I was going through.

I got close to my younger brother again, and he would bring his son and daughter over, which was a delight. They were three and five years old. So I had coloring books and colors for them, and on Easter we dyed eggs. I really enjoyed that!

Then my brother was going through some hard times, and ended up having a nervous breakdown. I did my best to encourage him, and help him with the stress in his life.

He ended up going away for a while, and since I didn't have a car anymore (it had broken down), I didn't get to see him for quite a while. After he got home I got to spend time with him again. Because I had my own experience with nervous breakdowns, I was able to encourage and strengthen him in his difficult time.

MEMOIRS:

March 30, 1990, Saturday

My roommate and I sat and talked about relationships. I talked about my old boyfriend and myself, that he says we're just best friends right now, but that I love him, and that even if we don't get back together, that I'll never be able to love anyone as I love him.

My roommate talked about her and her boyfriend, and that she knows that she could never marry him, but it's real hard for her to break up with him.

We discussed how difficult it is to find someone who hasn't been hurt deeply by a past relationship. That everyone has some scars from the past, and the problems that come with it.

So I told her that things will work out, one day at a time, and she said she knows that it will, that it'll just take time.

MEMOIRS:

April 6, Saturday 1990

My older sister and I spent every night together this week, Monday through Thursday.

I'm so lonely, and my life is so empty. I don't have any friends, and no man is interested in me at all. My life just seems so meaningless now! I don't know if I'll ever be a productive member of this society again. I feel real doubtful about ever going back to work. I have a mental illness and it keeps me from having friends, because of my mood swings.

I need someone to love. Will I be an old maid for the rest of my life? If I don't have my old boyfriend to love, then what's the use in being alive?

MEMOIRS:

April 25, Thursday, 1990

Its 3 a.m. I've been crying because I saw Quincy's (T.V. show) wedding. I am so lonely and sad lately. I keep thinking about the fact that no man ever loved me enough to want to share his life with me, to make the commitment of marriage. I've just been used like a grocery bag all my life by men. All they ever wanted was their own gratification, none of them ever cared about my feelings and needs. All they did was use me for their own selfish needs.

MEMOIRS:

May 16, Thursday, 1990

I see fat, ugly people who are married with kids, and I wonder what is wrong with me because I don't have a man who loves me. There must be something terribly wrong with me that I don't have anyone who loves me.

I became born again in February of 1991 and started a lot of socializing, bible study groups, new friends and Christian retreats; it went on for a year. It was so much fun meeting others who believed in God, and we shared so much. It changed my life forever!

I was able to end my relationship with my last boyfriend once and for all. Last time he called I told him that I didn't want him to ever call again, and I hung up so he couldn't protest and argue. I was free of him at last!

MEMOIRS:

December 18, 1990 Tuesday

I wrote my old boyfriend a letter saying that I hope his parents appreciate all the help he has given them, and that although America is the land of opportunity, people have to work their asses off to get what they want, nobody is just given anything.

I told him about my nephew and his wife, and about their daughter being born in Germany. I also told my old boyfriend about my nephew being in Saudi Arabia right now, and that if war breaks out he probably will fight because he is a heavy weapons expert.

MEMOIRS:

December 24, Monday 1990

Well, I have a couple things to do before my younger sister gets here at 2 o'clock. I have to finish my older sister's afghan. I finished half of the loose ends the other night. Then I have to wrap it.

My younger sister is bringing some wrapping paper for my older sister's present, and my younger sister's husband is going to come and watch my video of the Poseidon Adventure. I forgot I even had it. So I'm just relaxing now.

My sister and her husband kept me company while I made the cookies. I played my Christmas music. We had a nice time.

I took a shower, and fixed my hair, and put on makeup to look half decent. I couldn't get into my miniskirt, so I'm wearing my lavender sweatpants and pink sweater. That's about all I can wear. That's depressing. I'm pushing 180 pounds now. I have to lose weight; I can't stand being this fat!

I wrapped up all the cookies for Christmas, each person gets four cookies for Christmas, I hope they appreciate them. I myself don't care how much somebody spends on me; I just like the thought behind the present.

Since I've been poor, I don't expect anyone to spend a lot of money on me. What means the most to me is how people treat me. Loving and caring are worth more than any amount of money, and that's what really counts in life, loving and caring. There just isn't enough of that in life.

What people say and do are more worthy than millions of dollars! Being there when another person needs you is the most important thing in life. I learned that the hard way. My last boyfriend said he was always there for me- that is a bunch of baloney! When I was in the hospital recuperating from a near fatal overdose, all he did was bitch about how badly I treated him by taking the overdose; he didn't give a damn about my feelings. My feelings were never important to him-my feelings were just a nuisance to him-that's how self-centered he was! And I'll never forget that experience as long as I live!

When you think about it, that's a pretty sad life to live. That no matter how much pain you're going through, somebody else thinks they're suffering more.

MEMOIRS:

December 25, Thursday 1990

All day I just tried to ignore my older sister's boyfriend. It seems like I just can't like him. It's not because of the way he is, it's because he's with her, and she thinks she's in love with him. There is no doubt in my mind that he is the wrong person for her. She just can't see it-when she's "in love", her brain and common sense go out the window! I just don't want to see her get hurt again, like she always does.

Writing all this down has helped me to calm down. I guess it's because when I write my thoughts down, I have to get them organized, and they seem to make more sense than if they just keep running through my mind.

I'm glad I started this journal. I read through it now and then, and sometimes I'm embarrassed by what I wrote, but most of the time it helps me to see myself better, to see how I go through the trials of life, and I can see how much progress I make, and how I relapse at times.

MEMOIRS:

December 30, Sunday 1990

Reading "The Pilgrim's Progress" is really teaching me a lot about being a Christian. It tells about all the obstacles that can come in my way to make me feel like giving up God's way. I can't believe the changes I've been going through in just the past few days. It seems like I'm seeing things in a new way, through God's eyes.

These past few days I have been able to look back through the years at all the things I did, and how the things I thought were important weren't important at all. As a matter of fact, those things were taking me further away from God.

For instance, I went to college to increase my knowledge, because I always prided myself on my intelligence. But, the knowledge I gained was not godly knowledge, but worldly knowledge, and that means nothing to God. When we idolize our intelligence, it makes us proud and haughty. And those attitudes are sinful. That kind of intelligence can't comprehend believing in God. Now I long to gain the Lord's wisdom, for that will make me humble. It helps me to see just how unworthy I really am.

MEMOIRS:

December 31, Monday 1990

My old boyfriend called this afternoon and wished me happy New Year. He also told me more about his family and all the trouble that his younger brother is causing. His other brother is mad at that brother. He also said his dad is really suffering mentally because of all this turmoil.

MEMOIRS

January 5, Saturday 1991

I feel much more calm and serene. I don't get angry about insignificant things now. The only important things in life now are pertaining to God and how he wants me to live. I feel safe and protected because God is with me, and he is leading me on the right path.

Chapter Ten

A New Life

I started making a lot of new friends, and joined some bible studies. I went on a couple of Christian retreats, and I went to a Maranatha concert at the University.

I became a sponsor for a foreign couple and their daughter. We met at a church. I just wanted to give to others, so my pastor introduced me to them.

MEMOIRS:

August 21, Wednesday 1991

I got home at six p.m., an hour later than I had told the lady I would be. So I didn't hear from her until 8 p.m. Then she and her daughter came over, and I taught her English for an hour. She brought me some more food! We spent most of the hour reading a very short article in Time magazine, and we worked on pronunciation and the meanings of words, and also related words and subjects. I'm teaching her to divide words up into syllables, and practicing saying each syllable alone, and then putting it all together again.

Then I called the bookstore to see if they have a pronunciation book for ESL students. So she and I might go over there tomorrow morning, and see what they have that could help her in her studying.

She came over at 10 a.m. and we walked over to see if the bookstore had any books for her learning English.

She came over again around 5:30, and then a friend of mine stopped in. So she told her all about her family and all of us talked about it. Then my girlfriend left around 7:00, and I taught her some more English.

MEMOIRS:

August 25, Sunday 1991

Well, I was sick all day Saturday again. I went over to my friends for dinner, and visited with them. They showed me all their pictures and then we watched a video of their New Year's party before they came to America.

MEMOIRS:

August 28, Wednesday 1991

Monday morning my friend came over around 9:30 and we studied English a little and she was telling me about their customs, and she spoke a lot about her sons and the trouble between her husband and them. She left at noon, and I haven't heard from her since then. She was supposed to come over last night for more English, but she never called.

MEMOIRS:

September 1, Sunday 1991

The day started out like this: I met my friends for bible study, but found out it doesn't start until next Sunday, so we went back to my house. We read in the paper and talked. Then we went to the 10:30 service.

Saturday she and I went to the animal shelter to look at cats and dogs. Then I drove her to my hometown to show her where I grew up and went to school. Then we stopped at moms, and I showed her the house, and then we talked to mom and dad outside a little. Then we went to crossroads and she found the dictionary she wants to buy next week. Then we walked around the lake and she went home.

Well, I need to grow in my faith with the Lord, and I need to spend more time in nurturing that relationship. After talking to my male friend, I realize that I have been too busy thinking of others. Even though I spend hours every day studying God's word, I need to remember to use his power in my life to rebuke Satan, and learn and grow in his love, and to stop looking and trying to help others so much. I need to be strong in the Lord before I can go out and minister to others!

MEMOIRS:

September 4, Wednesday 1991

Then I went to Red Lobster and had good fellowship with friends from church. We just talked about things we're working on in our lives and trusting God to lead us.

September 15, Sunday 1991

At 7:30 my friend and her husband and daughter came over and they asked me to tape the summaries of the first two chapters in Data Processing for her.

MEMOIRS:

September 22, Sunday 1991

Then on Tuesday I went to the Bible study at church. And I went to the Bible study with my sister at her church that night. My friend had dropped off her book and tape recorder, so Wednesday I taped four chapters for her. She picked them up on Wednesday night, and told me about her car accident, so I made some calls to help her with it.

MEMOIRS:

September 27, Friday 1991

Today I made a bunch of phone calls. My friend's husband had stopped in last night, and told me about asking his teacher to take notes for him in one of his classes; so I called the Tutor Center today and asked them about types of help available for my friends. So I called her up at 11:00, and told her who to see there-I don't know if she did-I suppose I'll find out this weekend.

I was also spending time with my male friend, but we didn't hit it off. We were friends for a while and I was attracted to him, but he found somebody else. So life goes on!

MEMOIRS:

October 6, Sunday 1991

At 7:00 my friend came over for about 15 minutes, and I gave her the bible I bought for her and her husband. I also gave her the Portals of Prayer and told her how to use it. She was real happy with the bible, and thanked me a couple of times. I told her how I study the bible every morning before I go out.

MEMOIRS:

October 7, Monday 1991

My life is changing. I'm making some new friends and reestablishing my friendships with others, and I'm joining a Church, and making new friends there, and getting involved with their bible studies. I thank the lord for opening these doors for me. My life is becoming more active and balanced. I am feeling more content these past few days. I don't feel like I'm trapped as much as I used to. Now I have people that I can call and get together with when I feel like it. Praise the lord!

MEMOIRS:

October 18, Friday 1991

Also last night I called my friend to see how they are doing, and explained to her that I had been up north last weekend. They had asked me to go to the cities with them last Saturday, but I had forgotten that I was going up north, and then I couldn't get a hold of them.

MEMOIRS:

November 9, Saturday 1991

She and I went out to Crossroads-she let me drive. I had to get a bunch of things. We had a nice time. Then we came back here and talked for a while, and then I helped her with a paper for her English class. We talked a little more, and then she went home.

MEMOIRS:

November 29, Friday 1991

Wednesday I got up and I told myroommate that I'd wait to take a shower until she was done taking a bath and washing her hair. So in the meantime, I read God's word. But then she asked if she could do her laundry, and I said ok because I would be reading for another twenty minutes. But then when I wanted to take a shower (it was going on 12) she said she just started another load.

Now, she wasn't going anywhere on Thanksgiving Day, she was going to be alone. So I got angry and told her I wanted to take a shower this morning, and that she didn't say she was going to do two loads of laundry. And I asked her why she couldn't have done it on Thanksgiving day when she was going to be alone.

I was angry. She said, "well, what do you have to do anyway?" I said "For your information I have a busy day today!" And she said "You know the world doesn't revolve around you," and I said, "Well, it doesn't revolve around you either, but you sure act like it." She does! She's always doing stuff like that!

I spent a lot of time with family, going places and doing activities. I was pretty busy most of the time, but I still struggled with loneliness and depression. I also had been suffering from insomnia for a long time, which really messed up my days and nights.

MEMOIRS:

January 9, Thursday 1992

My younger brother called this morning around 9:40 and we talked until 11:10. We discussed solutions to his and his wife's problems, and he suggested that they get counseling individually. The Holy Spirit really opened my eyes-I saw two people who are hurting, and instead of dealing with their separate problems, they're taking out their hurt and frustration, and feelings of inadequacy out on each other, causing more problems, and making each other unhappy.

I told him that if each of us just loved one another, and thanked God for all he had given us, that we wouldn't hurt one another, or complain about the things we don't have.

I told him to cherish his family-to think of what his life would be like without them. I told him how it feels to be alone, and not have anyone here with me, and coming home to an empty house. He understood and saw what I was saying.

I told him how I thank the Lord for the safe and comfortable home I have. That I not only have everything I need, but much more! So it gave him and me a new perspective on life. That instead of taking things for granted, and complaining about things, that we should thank the Lord for all the abundant blessings he has lavished on us. Praise be to the Lord! Amen!! And let me remember this every hour of my life, and I'll be at peace with God's love! Hallelujah!

MEMOIRS:

January 22, Wednesday 1992

So I don't know what's been happening to me for the last couple months. Why have I been so cut off from others, and why do I keep hoping that my old boyfriend and I can get back together-and why do I miss that relationship so much?

He was my dearest friend-we stood side-by-side through good times and bad times. We grew up together. We helped each other when the other was weak. We encouraged and uplifted one another. We had a bond so strong. We knew each other inside and out. Since we've been apart, I feel like a part of me is missing. All the hopes and dreams we had together were dashed. The thing that damaged our relationship was our living 80 miles apart. A relationship has to be physically together-we talked on the phone almost every day for two years, but without being there to touch, and hug, and talk for long periods of time-or just the fact of having the other person physically near makes you stronger. Talking for a few minutes together on the phone is far from the needed intimacy of hugging, or just sitting, or lying together reading or watching TV.

So for the next year I spent a lot of time doing things with family-mom and dad, my younger sister and her husband, and with my other sister, and with my brother. And so life went on.

My friends graduated from college and moved to the city and we lost touch.

MEMOIRS:

March 27, 1992

Nobody ever feels sorry for me, or offers to help me in anyway. I am treated like shit over and over. No one ever asks, "hey can I do anything to help you?" Never, ever!

So what am I living for? I lost my career, I lost my true love, I lost my ability to work, I lost every friend I ever had, and I have even lost myself. I don't have any idea of who I am, or what I am here for.

People who I thought cared about me haven't seen me in months, but they don't even bother calling me. I don't know what keeps me going from day-to-day-I really don't. One day just melts into another, endlessly, meaninglessly.

The only way I know the passing of time is when night comes and when the sun shines in the morning. Some days start with a glimmer of hope, but it eventually fades. I feel as if I'm imprisoned by my own mind! And that has to be the worst any human can feel. Because how can you escape from your own mind?

......what happened to the person who was full of hope and life and looked forward to making a difference in the world? What happened to the feisty fighter in me that said, "I will survive!"? I don't know, and I don't know if that old self will ever come back. You see, I don't even have myself to rely on any more. What does a person do when they lose themselves? What comes after that?

June 1992 a new roommate, moved in and through her I met a new guy.

MEMOIRS:

June 6, Sunday 1992

Sunday night my new roommate and her friends went to the bar. I ended up dancing with one guy for most of the night. We danced really well together. I felt really comfortable with him. He taught me a new step and I taught him one.

He came over Tuesday night, at 6 p.m., and he and my new roommate and I talked together for a couple hours. Then he and I walked around the lake and talked about things we've done and the usual stuff you talk about when you're getting to know someone.

When we got back from our walk, we sat on my couch and talked about ourselves and we talked about how we felt when we danced together, and when we hugged and kissed. I feel pretty comfortable with him. I told him that we need to just get to know each other slowly. (He was 48 years old, and I was 38 years old). I have a lot of mixed emotions about this new relationship. I'm afraid to really open myself up, because I did that with others, and it caused me so much heartache.

I know that I'm different now, gaining wisdom from God, and that he may or may not be the person I've seen so far. It is really hard for me. He seems so gentle and sensitive, but so did other men in my life (at the beginning of the relationships).

MEMOIRS:

July 7, Tuesday 1992

He and I went to the park and sat in the van and talked for almost two hours. We both talked about our fears, about how we felt our relationship is progressing-whether it's been going too fast. We each feel comfortable about it.

We discussed the need to spent time with our friends also, so that our relationship doesn't become exclusive, which wouldn't be very healthy. We've been doing that.

With him, I feel like a woman-he treats me like a woman, and that's something new for me. It's also scary, because it means I have responsibility in the relationship, and I don't have much experience having that. I was always treated like a little girl by other men. So I shared that with him.

MEMOIRS:

August 2, Sunday 1992

Then around 11:45 he called from home and I asked him what happened. And he said again that he doesn't feel worthy of my love, and he doesn't know how to deal with it because he's never had that before.

MEMOIRS:

September 11, Friday 1992

He just called and said he's going to be busy all night. I was disappointed and I told him, and I'm angry (he'd been making all kinds of excuses for the last couple months). I feel like I've just been being used these last few months. I'm ready to end this relationship. I don't need to baby another man, and tolerate his uncaring and irresponsible behavior. I'm not going to put up with it anymore-enough is enough!

The first month we went together he was taking me out to eat almost every day, and now it's just once in a while, and it's only at cheap fast food places. Now lately he says he's broke, so what made the difference?

Why do I keep doing the same thing over and over again? Maybe because I want to believe that there is at least one man on this earth that is capable of loving fully and being caring about my needs and feelings. This has made me cry. I feel like my head is breaking into a million pieces.

MEMOIRS:

October 22, Thursday 1992

Tuesday night he called, I wasn't sure if he was going to or not. I cried for quite a while before he called. I've been feeling so sad lately, and thinking about all the things I won't ever have in my life. Like getting married and having kids, and having a house and just a "normal" life like all my cousins did.

I know I keep thinking these things over and over, and it just opens up all those wounds, and the pain feels just as strong now as in the past, and in some respects it's even a deeper pain, because I know that for every day that goes by means one less day in which those things I want are passing me by.

It's been so hard for me to write because of these intense feelings, and if I don't write, then I usually don't have to think about it.

I guess all I really want is to have a husband who truly loves me, and is gentle and considerate to me-is that too much to ask?

MEMOIRS:

December 14, Monday 1992

Well, I talked to my new boyfriend twice tonight about our relationship. We've only been seeing each other when he feels like it.

I am deeply hurt and angry. I feel like I've been used by him. When things start getting serious, he runs. So I asked him what his intentions were he didn't have an answer.

I am feeling angry, lonely, spiteful and revengeful. I found out he is just like every other man-egocentric, and selfish. What pisses me off the most is that he just agrees with everything I say about him. That's how little he cares. He doesn't even try to stand up for himself-that makes me sick! That's spineless!

On May 3, 1993, I ended up in treatment because of an overdose. After twenty eight days, I went to another city to live at a treatment center for women. I was there from June to December of 1993.

MEMOIRS:

July 6, Tuesday 1993

I feel so helpless about my disease of alcoholism, and I look at all the things that I've lost because of it, including myself. I have so much sadness inside because of these things. I guess I'm feeling a lot of grief, and I have a lot of things to mourn to get healthy. I was going to say get healthy again, but I've never really been healthy before, so it's going to take a lot of work and determination.

I'm afraid to try again for fear of failing. I'm afraid of living, but I don't really want to die. So what do I do? I don't want to just be going through the motions. I want my life to be real to me. God, bless me with your strength to do whatever I need to, to get better, to get in touch with my feelings as often as I can, that should be all the time. But I can't expect myself to change overnight. I need to be gentler with myself, and to take care of myself.

MEMOIRS:

December 1, 1993

I moved into my apartment by a lake. It was nice having my own space. All I had was a boom box for music and cassette tapes, and a table and a chair. Oh, I also had an air mattress to sleep on. All my stuff was in storage in my hometown. I worked in customer service at Woolworth's.

MEMOIRS:

December 9, Thursday 1993

I ate dinner and read my novel for a while, but the stress and feeling of not being able to make it became overwhelming. I lay down in bed and cried for a little while. I felt like I was losing my mind again, like I had on Sunday. But I cried and prayed. I feel so lonely and tired. I didn't feel like I could do this living thing.

I felt torn between wanting to quit my job, and not having any money if I did. And I felt like running away, just leaving, but I know that wherever I go, there I'll be, so it isn't a choice. My healthy side is stronger than my addict side. So I just cried because there is no way to get away from life! Isn't that a bitch! Last night I was feeling so defeated and overwhelmed at the thought of how I'm going to get my things here, and with whom, ad infinitum, that I even thought of just going back home next month. Life is very difficult for me. I'm 38 years old, and I don't know how to live! That is sad and overwhelming for me at times!

I still had contact with my old boyfriend occasionally and I was trying to get my things like TV and VCR from my last boyfriend.

MEMOIRS:

December 26, Sunday

I am so grateful. I have a job I like with co-workers who are very nice, I have a nice apartment and everything I need, and I'm making more friends in AA. Things are really getting better in my life, and it's because of God's love and grace, that I'm learning to live sober for the first time in my life. God is very good to me!

On February 28, 1994, my old boyfriend moved to California, so he gave me the car that we had bought in the city. So I had wheels again! After four and a half years of walking and bussing! For the first month I only drove the car to work and back and gradually started driving more and more.

On April 20 I packed up my car, with help from friends. And I left for home. I stayed at mom and dads for $150 a month. I got a

Programmer Analyst job at a company on the day after Memorial Day. I moved to a new apartment on July first, 1994,a beautiful apartment.

Things went quite normal for a couple of months, and then the depression came in. I started suffering anxiety attacks and poor self-esteem. I didn't feel like I fit at work and I started isolating. I ended up in the hospital in October from a nervous breakdown again. My life just seemed like a black hole. And when I went back to work my boss was concerned about medications I was taking. It just wasn't good, people were unfriendly before this and now it was even worse since I "went off the deep end." I eventually ended up getting let go. So there I was again! I had tried again and lost again! So I ended up on long-term disability for two years. I was still sober and I kept myself busy with projects like crocheting Afghans.

I had a really nice apartment and plenty of money, but I was alone, and I was ready to have a relationship with the right person.

I worked all kinds of temporary jobs and I worked at a computer factory. I met a guy there. The first thing he asked me (after he saw my diamond rings) was "How many times have you been married?", and I said "none". Then later he asked me if I'd like to go out for coffee after work, which was 11:30 p.m. I said "maybe" and thought about it.

So we started going to Perkins after work each night after work, and got to know a little about each other. And he told me that he could tell that I'd been hurt in the past. He seemed like a good person, but I was to find out his weakness of gambling in a big way.

My long-term disability was ending in a few months, and I was going to need help with rent and utilities. He was living with his brother and sister in-law and he was working in his brother's body shop days and then worked at the computer factory at night, so I got the feeling that he was a hard worker. Boy was I wrong.

He moved in with me and then he started missing work and finding reasons not to work. Well, I had a five thousand dollar C.D. in the bank, and I started borrowing from it each month. We were playing bingo very often and losing money like crazy. Six months later my C.D. was gone, zilch! Five thousand gone from gambling and taking off from work! What a mess!

So June of 1997 we had to move to a cheaper apartment. It took us four days to move! I had never moved in more than a few hours before. And I had moved many times over the years.

So I ended up paying for everything with my disability check each month. Our life together was a joke. If we were working and had money, he'd be gambling, playing bingo. Otherwise he'd spend the whole day putzing in the garage. I had asked him to move out I don't know how many times! He wouldn't go and I was ready to explode! Something had to give!

He owed me over $20,000 for rent and other expenses that I had paid for him. Then he finally got a VA Pension. But he never paid me back for all those years that he had stuck me with the bills.

He finally paid his share of expenses, but nothing more. Just around that time in 2003, I had quit drinking, and started attending AA. I was going to a meeting every day, and made a few friends. Life was improving, but I was still miserable.

Now that I was sober I saw what a wreck our relationship was. He just did whatever he pleased and we were going nowhere. He became jealous of the time I was spending at AA and with new friends.

We had lived in our apartment for ten years and there came the time when we couldn't renew our lease, so we started looking for an apartment. All he did was find fault with every apartment we looked at. It was hell! I didn't have enough money to get a place of my own, so I was stuck with him.

We found an apartment for people fifty-five plus, and the building was nice, a dining room, a community room, a lobby, and there were potlucks and other activities. So November 20, 2007 we started moving in. He wanted to move us with his truck, so we ended up moving for six weeks.

This was a place I had been interested in for forty years; there was never a riverside apartment available before now. So here we were moving in and all he did was find fault. He didn't like the people that sat in the lobby and gossiped about others; that they just try to get information about us so they could gossip, and on, and on. He was starting to ruin my happiness about finally being here.

So all those years with him were nothing but poverty and gambling. And then he had taken over all the household chores, including picture hanging, and curtain hanging, which I loved. He wouldn't let me do anything, and yet he criticized the artistic work I did, and my reading books. So when he died it was a shock, now I had the freedom to do anything, but I also had to do everything all by myself. When you're with someone 24/7 for eleven and a half years, it's a shock when they are gone. Nothing from nothing leaves nothing. I soon learned that "that which does not kill me makes me stronger." It was a long haul.

To show you the dilemma I found myself in, read the poetry I wrote about losing him:

"His Death"

Incredible!

Him lying there lifeless.

Total wrenching of my heart,

Pleading for God to bring him back!

Emptiness, Loneliness, Numb,

Confusion-what do I do now?

Meaninglessness,

Cold, so cold!

No warm and fuzzy bear hugs

I'll never feel again it hurts too much!

Entering my abode there is no voice to greet me.

No one to comfort me!

I hug myself and I cry like I've never cried before.

Loud sobs.

Hugging my body.

Rocking forward, then backward.

Time seems endless......

My old boyfriend and I kept in touch until late 2008. After my last boyfriend died I had called him and asked if he could help me financially, and he said "Why don't you ask one of your other boyfriends?" So I cut off communicating with him right then and there with a letter. So that was the end of my thirty-two year relationship with him.

Chapter Eleven

Finding Myself

After my last boyfriend died I went through a period of finding myself using poetry. Here are some excerpts:

POETIC MEMOIRS:

October 23, 2012

Well, the ending of another day is here. It amazes me how many different emotions I go through in a day. From peaceful, after studying God's word, to despair of how I am not treated with care, or respect, or concern by people around me. I feel like I keep getting trampled on, and it's like I can't seem to find a way out of this negative space.

Talking to a lady tonight, I realized that I am stronger and more resilient than I tend to think about myself. I need to give myself more credit! I've been through a lot in fifty seven years, and I'm still here, and I still have my faculties, unlike some unfortunates, and I've been remarkably resilient as to my emotions, my goals, and my dreams.

And I realized right now that I don't have to, and I don't need to let those negatives hold me down any longer. I still have life to live, and I need, and I want to find out what to do with the rest of my life. I need to find out "what life (and God) is expecting from me" quote by Victor Frankl in "Mans Search for Meaning", not what I'm expecting from life. Because that is exactly what has kept me from growing. Life always lets me down, one way or another, so why keep hitting my head against the wall?

Start looking at what life is expecting of me! God has been so generous with me, all the abilities and talents he has blessed me with. Maybe I need to start sharing those gifts with others who need them!

I just started studying poetry tonight. It just seemed the right time to start on a new journey to add to all my other talents. Old is going (but not gone), and the new is to revive my spirit, and to get a new perspective on life, and myself, and others. Maybe on this new quest God will give me wisdom on why people do the things they do.

POETIC MEMOIRS:

October 24, Wednesday

Well, I vented my pain and frustration about neighbors to my social worker. I need to reconcile myself to a life that doesn't run the way I think it should. When I can be reconciled, I will be more at peace, and I will stop my emotional upheavals that don't do anything good for me.

The Wednesday meeting was great! It was about just what I wrote, not taking people's hurtful words or actions personally. To be able to pray for them, because obviously, they are not healthy inside, they don't know how they hurt others.

I have to give up this "revenge" feeling I have, that "they" should know (be told) how they hurt me and pay for that hurt. This also does me no good!

It's always such a nice group to be with. People who like me, and enjoy my company, these are the type of people I need to spend time with. Positive, caring people. I need to leave the other in the dust, and not to take in their negativity and poison.

POETIC MEMOIRS:

October 24, 2012

As I'm reading, "Write Personal Poetry", it just occurred to me that maybe this loneliness, and the pain it causes, should not be perceived by me. Why do I accept this idea that I need to be liked or loved by others? When I think about it, I enjoy being by myself and I like my own company. It's peaceful and serene for the most part!

But putting this demand on my psyche only causes pain, because that's what expectations do to me. I really do enjoy just "being", and I can include another person into my world whenever it hits me!

After all, I am never alone; God lives in me, in my spirit, through his spirit. So why whip myself when I have the creative God that made me!

POETIC MEMOIRS:

October 25, Thursday

I'm sitting here by the window watching it snow, big, heavy flakes coming down swiftly on the wings of the wind. And I see how the wind is tickling the trees. I believe trees love wind, it stirs their branches in a private dance, praising the Lord for his love for them! The wind gives the trees energy, which helps them to spread out and grow, and reach up to God.

As a child, one day at school we were having recess and it was snowing. I just stood still and the movements of the snow made me feel like I was floating, like the snow was carrying me. And of course, I've felt that feeling a million times over the years, the decades.

When snow falls, it makes the lightest, tiniest sound. Did you ever notice that? A boat just went by on the river! That must be a unique experience, floating down the river with the snow swirling around you, landing on your face, accumulating on your eyelashes (or trying to).

POETIC MEMOIRS:

October 27, Saturday

    Things I see outside my window that someone else might not notice:

- the surface of the Mississippi river today is very tight, small, coarse ripples,
- the wind is rushing the water southward,
- the branches of the oak trees are more jagged and fewer than the Elm trees
- the branches of the Elm trees reach up and are very fine and full branches
- the river is being blown by a south wind now, and it's glassy with wider and smoother waves,
- How the sun keeps moving, shining on the trees at every angle, from dawn to dusk-every minute is a different picture,
- how I can see the sunrise (I face west) reflected in the windows of the hotel across the river,
- all the different hues of the sunset each day, each moment-the pinks, roses, purples, yellows, etc.,
- in the winter, the black outlines of the trees against the sky, especially as the sun sets.

Sounds that bring back memories:

- train whistles, all different kinds
- train engine idling
- water lapping against the shore,
- classical music, many artists, different tempos, etc.

- clock ticking tick-tock
- birds chirping and singing
- thunder
- light rain falling,
- pouring rain,
- the sound of squirrels chasing each other as they grapple onto the trees, and twirling around the trees,
- a cat's meow
- cat's purring

POETIC MEMOIRS:

November 8, Thursday

Feelings of déjà vu:

- when I see the word "olive" as a color, it stirs something deep inside of me and it seems to come from childhood, in grade school, something about the color "olive"
- when I hear the cars driving across the two bridges (I live between them), I can tell how cold, or wet, or dry the road surface is. The colder the temp outside, the higher and "whinier" the sound is,
- if it's raining out, it sounds "wet"
- if it's snowing out, it sounds "slushy"
- when it's hot outside, the sound is wider and more diffuse,
- when I walk through dry leaves, I love the muffled "crunch", and the sound of leaves brushing and crushing each other,
- in the fall when the acorns have fallen off the oak trees, I love the loud "crunch" sound they make, and the reverberations going through my foot.

POETIC MEMOIRS:

March 4, 2013

Describing things I hear:

- as I listen to yo yo ma's cello playing, it just makes me sway to the melody. It is so evocative, so full of feeling. But there's something about it that creates sad, heavy feelings. I used to like music like that years ago, when I was depressed, and was working on hard issues in my life.

But somehow, I'm not really enjoying it that way right now I don't like those heavy feelings. I turned it off, I feel lighter somehow, and I like the free feeling, almost like I can float if I wanted to.

Somewhere in the last year (maybe less), I've been getting a lot of déjà vu's-they only stay a few seconds-just long enough to actually remember a situation.

Little things-like the gesture of someone's hand will catch the edge of my memory, and when I try to recall the exact moment back in time, it's gone.

POETIC MEMOIRS:

A Dream of Belonging
That empty, hollow feeling
There is always a wall there
I can never get over the wall
No one ever invites me in.

WHAT IT TAKES TO FIND YOUR TRUE LOVE

I came out of your body, but
I've never been a part of you
My birth was quick and quite
Painless, you said.
I wonder if I just wanted to get out of that prison
You wished I would die, but I lived
All these years I keep wondering why-what keeps me here?
You didn't or don't want me to be here
I haven't really wanted to be here
I keep trying to be a part of, but it never happens

I am flesh of your flesh, but
No-one in the family has ever
Made me feel accepted or wanted

Family just finds fault with me
Every chance they get
I'm the one that should "pay"
For whatever I eat or use, no one else
Life is lonely, always lonely
I keep doing things to make life worthwhile, but it's all meaningless
I've come to the conclusion that even God doesn't want
me-why does he keep me here in this lonely world with no
one to love me? What kind of God would do that?

There is nothing in or on this world that I care about

Life is just meaningless! The people that have always
treated me the worst are my own flesh and blood.

BONNIE

I have never been afraid of death-death is a good
thing-no more toil, or strife-peace!

Any "love" I've ever felt was a tight constricting coil
that would just squeeze the life out of me.

For a large portion of my life (I'm 57), I have felt like I shouldn't have lived at this time. Most of my life, I've felt that I belonged to ages past, when women were women and men were men.

How can I describe it? It's hard to put into words. It's like I belong in the old days when women wore long puffy dresses, and hair was made up of nice curls and ringlets. When people walked on dirt roads, and horses and buggies took them where they needed to go.

Often I have wished that my ancestors hadn't come here to America. I often dreamed (daydreamed) of how life would have been there.

POETIC MEMOIRS:

Sometimes…..

I wonder how I would feel if I had no physical pain;
I wonder how I would feel being a concert pianist, or a harp player;
I dream about living in Paris;
I love reading comic books, and laughing so hard that tears come to my
    eyes, and I have difficulty catching my breath;
I like to be outlandish, and make others laugh;
I like to see the whimsy of everyday life,
I like burning incense because it brings back fond memories;

I love to wear perfume for the way it makes me feel feminine, and sometimes delights others;

I wish grandma was still here so I could ask her about her life, which I didn't think to ask her when I was young;

I wish my dad was still here, so I could tell him how his wisdom and humor touched my life;

I like to imagine living in a huge mansion on the edge of the ocean;

I wish that I could find some (or at least one) women friends that share similar lifestyles (no husbands, no children);

I wish people would be kinder and more thoughtful and understanding to me;

I think of chucking it all, and traveling wherever my will takes me.

POETIC MEMOIRS:

Poetry and Spirituality

- About practicing accepting things just as they are happening, not judging, just experiencing.
- I'm excited to see how my life unfolds.
- I've been on a four year quest to refind myself.
- I'm on a new and exciting path.
- Learning to accept things as they happen.
- Observing life and relaxing.
- More calmness and naturalness, not forcing or expecting.
- This living is so much easier.

MEMOIRS:

July 3, 2013

I'm so alone, Lord-I know I have you, but I cannot see you, or touch you, or feel you. I need comforting, Lord! Like that one psalm says, "No one cares for my soul, Lord, not one.

When no one cares, I just feel empty and I feel let down, Lord, because you and I know that I don't deserve this kind of treatment.

What did I do to these people who shun me? Nothing! People don't even try to get to know me, yet I see them congregating with others. What is this secret society? And why am I never included, Lord?

It hurts so bad that I can't even find words to describe my grief and loneliness.

God, I just want to be with you! I hate this world and everything in it, because all this world does is cause me pain!

Please God, take me to be with you! I've lived long enough and seen enough-please, bless me with your love and peace, and please take me to be with you! That is all I want, Lord-nothing else!!

I love you Lord and all I want is to be by your side.

I can't live in a world without love-I just can't do it anymore! I am tired and used up and empty. I have given all I have for nothing, obviously.

All the love, and tenderness, and empathy, and compassion, and encouragement, and everything I had, Lord, has been wasted for nothing.

The people I became spent from didn't deserve one damn iota of it! What a damn fool I've been. Caring for and doing all this for people who don't have any love in their hearts.

I gave without thinking of what I would get, and look how my life has turned out-I'm alone in this world with no one to care for me!

Three weeks later:

POETIC MEMOIRS:

July 22, 2013

My Castle

I love to sit here and look at my Christmas lights peeking through the beautiful lace curtains. The white blinds are closed so that they reflect the colored lights also.

It gives me a "dreamy" feeling. The lights also reflect on the glass doors of my barrister bookcases. This is my castle, one I created from lifelong dreams what I wanted to have around me.

Over time, years, I add new decorations to this atmosphere. The latest one is a clear, tubular vase, about a foot high, filled with colored glass baubles, done in rows or tiers of varying colors, river rocks (white), green, ecru, red, white, or clear marbles, etc.

It, they, just sparkle with reflected light, and with varying depths of colors.

My clocks here in the dining room are ticking away, slowly, beat by beat, like my heart. I have been practicing and learning to be aware of the present moment. And I try to refrain from thinking of all the "other" things I could be doing right now, instead of what I am doing. But, when I enjoy each moment, I learn a lot about myself, about what I think and feel about life. When I am "rushing" and "doing", and not enjoying the moment, I just feel stressed, and tired, and frustrated, and regretful!

Life is so much better when I just "dig in", and let things unfold as they may! I gain so much insight into the world, and life, and the meaning of life!

"The greatest love of all is happening to me", that beautiful song by Whitney Houston. The greatest love of all is inside of me-Jesus lives in my spirit, and when I obey God, I let him lead me and guide me in the way to go. In my spirit, I am always young, looking at life through my inner-child's eyes, but, physically I have to cope with an aging body, which can frustrate my spirituality (when I allow it to). And then I feel old and tired.

It's amazing the change and impact a little twinkling lights have on perception. "All things bright and beautiful..." how true! How such a small thing can change the ambience of a home!

Sometimes they bring back memories of childhood Christmas Eves, the only time mom and dad left the tree lights on overnight! Peace and happiness!

Chapter Twelve

Finding My Soul mate

After all these years of soul-searching, I was still stuck. Depression kept gnawing at me, and discontent with my life. I was tired of being alone, and began to feel ready for someone to come into my life.

All the years I spent searching for some friend, some companion that would love the Lord like I did and who could lift me up when I'm down. And after fifty eight years I found him-my husband. We found each other and we found what we were looking for. Thank you, God!

He asked if he could talk to me about something that was bothering him. So he came over, and we talked, and I gave him my advice about a relationship he was ending.

He had moved into the building in March and we had talked a little bit here and there is passing, and I had heard people here talk about things he was doing and everybody liked him.

I had had a lonely summer, and I was ready for a friend. He wrote me a thank you letter for our visit. I thought that was really sweet. He started taking me to doctor visits (I had come down with anemia), and he took me shopping.

He came over every night after work to talk and visit and he didn't make any moves on me, which really impressed me! He was a real gentleman, and I loved the little letters he'd leave on my door!

This guy was very special, and we began spending more time together. He asked me in a letter if I would make a list of twelve things I wanted from a man, and he had written a list of twelve things he wanted from a woman.

This was my kind of guy! I had been thinking about this very subject for the last couple of years, so I made my list. And when we exchanged our lists, we found we were looking for the same things! He had just finished writing a book about his overcoming depression. We were meant to be together!

Here are the lists we made:

Twelve Things That I Need In My Life from a Man

1. Kindness
2. Sense of humor
3. Generous with self and others
4. Helpful
5. Playful
6. Friendship
7. Confidante
8. Open and honest
9. Gentle, yet firm
10. Encouraging
11. Resourceful
12. Romantic
13. Appreciative
14. Grateful
15. Imaginative
16. Share cooking and housework

My Needs in the World: His list

- Someone to talk to when life is getting to rough.
- Someone to depend upon in tough times when I am suffering.
- Someone to have coffee with in the morning, very important to me.
- Someone to have fun with, such as: fishing, or playing cards, or going out to eat.
- Someone that cares about me, and I mean really care.

- Someone I can trust, trust, trust!
- Someone to listen to me when I'm talking.
- Someone that can cook supper and be happy doing it.
- Someone that will accept me the way I am.
- Someone without so much baggage in life that it interferes with our life.
- Someone who can go to the Catholic Church with me every Sunday.
- Someone to lay next to at night and just keeps me warm and not have to talk.

MEMOIRS:

November 11, Monday 2013

He and I started talking one week before Labor Day. He wrote me some letters at first-I wrote a few to him, and our relationship just blossomed! He's moved in with me-started in October.

He and I had started out real slow-small conversations here and there. He started spending more time with me-we had both gone through a difficult summer, both experiencing depression, and wishing we were gone, to be honest with you. But we reached out to each other and found that we were looking for the same things, and we just slowly melded together. I don't know how else to describe it-we were meant for each other and neither one of us had ever felt this kind of love before. We were a blessing for each other! God is so good!

Today he got the first hardback and softcover books that he wrote! Finally, after five years of hard work and planning! We also celebrated Veteran's Day-we ate at Applebee's (he got a free meal).

He is a wonderful person, and he is so loving to me! I am so happy that we got together. I had been talking to him coming and going since February or March.

MEMOIRS:

December 2, 2013 Monday

Inspiration

Meeting my new love has awakened my heart. My heart has come out of its coma, and I feel happy and alive for the first time in my life!

My love is something new, never felt before. It's scary because it's new, but it's invigorating, like a spring rain. We feel like we are one, we mesh in our love.

His presence makes my heart sing! His presence brings a peaceful feeling, and I feel safe and secure. His love wraps around my heart like a beautiful fog in wintertime. It envelopes me.

I feel at peace when I can get away from fretting and worrying, and when I remember that the Lord is in control of everything.

Life has meaning again, and the future looks bright and new! I am excited, and a little scared because I've never known this feeling before, nor had I ever had someone who truly loved me before!

Thank you, Lord, for blessing me, and taking care of me in such a compassionate and tender way!

I love you, Lord, and I love my love.

So you see, if you hold on and trust in the Lord, miracles can happen! Just hold on during the storm and keep your faith, and your dreams will come true! I never thought I'd find the kind of man I was looking for, and he just walked into my life-forever. Praise the Lord!

Every time he caresses me or puts his loving arms around me, I think "this is what love is", after all these years and after all the counterfeits! This is love-how wonderful. My dream has finally come true!

References

2Timothy 4:16,17 Nelsons NKJV Study Bible

Frankl, V. Man's Search for Meaning, 3rd ed. Pocket Books, New York, 1984.

The write start: a guide to nurturing writing at every stage, from scribbling to forming letters and writing stories/ Jennifer Halllissy.

Quote from Whitney Houston "Greatest Love of All" song

God willing, the things we do and say can make us spend more time gathering our thoughts about what we've accomplished in our lives. We feel an urge to escape from insanity and take a new road to recovery that brings us to who we really are. I know the things that the (author) has overcome again and again. I think she's in a great position to give sound judgment to others, as she has come a long way. Her journey brings hope and prosperity, leaving no stone unturned.

- younger brother

The author of this book has been a longtime friend, and she has hit the nail on the head when she says that when you wait on the Lord he will bring you the one true love that's right for you.

-lifetime friend

This is a wonderful story of a lady who had a lot of hardships and difficulties on a rocky road, and she managed to get through them and found her mate.

Ron and Barb friends and neighbors

I feel the writer is a courageous woman who has lived a hard life. It's always nice to see a happy ending to a story of someone's life who truly deserves it. It inspires me to see someone who can lay out their lives for others to take a look at to learn and understand. I am grateful I could share her experiences through her book.

- a friend

Sometimes in life we get so many chances to change what we really need to change, like fruitless relationships and hanging around negative people which keeps us down. Yesterday is gone, we cannot change the past, but we can change today and the way we live. In June and July of 2013 both of us were at a low point, but we didn't know each other yet. By writing her book my wife has become stronger emotionally, mentally and more at peace with her life. Her book gives inspiration, hope and perseverance for people struggling with relationships. Today my wife and I have a happy and wonderful life together, which includes reading the Bible every day.

-Husband and Author of "Losing the Will to Live, Why?"

Edwards Brothers Malloy
Oxnard, CA USA
January 5, 2016